The Pizza That We Made

by Joan Holub • *illustrated by* Lynne Cravath

VIKING

For Mom and Dave,
two pizza-lovers—J.H.
For Jeff, the great chef—L.C.

VIKING BOOKS
Published by the Penguin Group
Penguin Putnam Books for Young Readers,
345 Hudson Street, New York, New York 10014, U.S.A.

Penguin Books Ltd, Registered Offices: Harmondsworth, Middlesex, England

First published in the United States of America
by Viking and Puffin Books, divisions of Penguin Putnam
Books for Young Readers, 2001

1 3 5 7 9 10 8 6 4 2

Text copyright © Joan Holub, 2001
Illustrations copyright © Lynne Cravath, 2001
All rights reserved

LIBRARY OF CONGRESS CATALOGING-IN-PUBLICATION DATA
Holub, Joan.
The pizza that we made / by Joan Holub ; pictures by Lynne Cravath.
p. cm. — (Viking easy-to-read) (Puffin easy-to-read. Level 2)
Summary: Three young cooks have fun making their own pizza, cleaning up
their mess, and eating hot slices!
ISBN 0-670-03520-3 (hardcover)—ISBN 0-14-230019-5 (pbk.)
[1. Pizza—Fiction. 2. Cookery—Fiction. 3. Stories in rhyme.]
I. Cravath, Lynne Woodcock, ill. II. Title. III. Series.
IV. Series: Puffin easy-to-read. Level 2
PZ8.3.H74 Pi 2001   [E]—dc21   2001000111

Viking® and Easy-to-Read® are registered trademarks of Penguin Putnam Inc.

Printed in Hong Kong

Reading Level 2.3

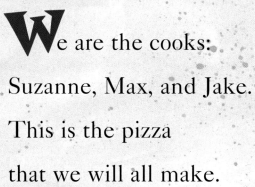

We are the cooks:
Suzanne, Max, and Jake.
This is the pizza
that we will all make.

This is the way
that we begin.
These are the things
that we will add in.

This is the flour,

so soft and fine.

This is the cup
we fill to the line.

This is the mix
we stir with a spoon.

This is the way

we sing a fun tune.

These are our hands
that mash and fold.

These are our fingers
that push and mold.

This is our bowl.

It's just the right size.

In goes the dough.

It's starting to rise!

This is the way

we make the dough fly.

We toss it down low.

We toss it up high.

This is the dough
we spread in the pan.

This is the sauce

we pour from a can.

These are the green things
we chop, chop, chop.

This is the cheese

that goes on top.

This is the oven

we use to cook.

This is the window.

Let's all take a look!

This is the mess

that we clean away.

We wipe. We sweep.

We're done. Hooray!

This is the way

the table is set.

Where is the pizza?

Is it ready yet?

This is the clock.

There goes the bell.

Sniff. Sniff. Mmmm.

What a great smell!

This is our pizza.

It's ready to eat.

It tastes so yummy.

What a great treat!

These are the crusts

left on each plate.

This *was* the pizza

that we all ate.

Make your own pizza!

(Ask an adult for help using sharp tools or the oven.)

WHAT YOU WILL NEED FOR THE DOUGH:

2/3 cup warm water
1 teaspoon active dry yeast
1/2 teaspoon sugar
1/2 teaspoon salt
1 tablespoon oil (olive oil is best)
1 2/3 cups flour

1. Preheat oven to 400 degrees.
2. Mix yeast and water in a bowl.
3. Stir in sugar, salt, and oil.
4. Slowly mix in flour.
5. Knead dough on a lightly floured, clean surface for 2 minutes.
6. Place dough ball in a bowl and cover. Let it rise in a warm place for 45 minutes.
7. With greased hands, spread dough to fill a lightly oiled 12-inch pizza pan.

WHAT YOU WILL NEED FOR THE TOPPINGS:

3/4 cup pizza sauce
1 cup grated mozzarella cheese
Vegetables such as green peppers, tomatoes, broccoli, onions, mushrooms

1. Spread sauce on the dough.
2. Chop vegetables and put them on top of the sauce.
3. Sprinkle cheese over everything.
4. Bake pizza for 15 to 25 minutes or until it looks done.

Enjoy!

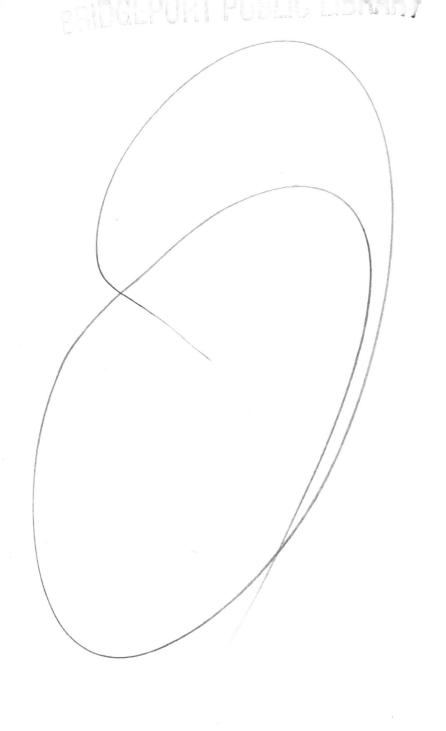